To kylie,

My Texas Buddy!

Paul D. Epner

12/11/03

Inquires should be addressed to Imaginative Publishing, Ltd., Attention: Permissions Department, P. O. Box 150008, Fort Worth, TX 76108.

email: information@imaginativepublishing.com
website: www.imaginativepublishing.com

ISBN 0-9743335-3-0 (previously ISBN 1-57168-678-9)

10 9 8 7 6 5 4 3 2 1   01 02 03 04 05

First Imaginative Publishing, Ltd. edition, August 2003

Printed and bound in Hong Kong

Herbert Hilligan's Lone Star Adventure

Written by Paul Epner

Illustrated by Vuthy Kuon & Duke Nguyen

IMAGINATIVE PUBLISHING • Fort Worth, Texas

I dedicate this book, I recently penned,
To Susan, my wife—and lifelong friend.

And to Allison my daughter in all her glory
Be healthy, happy, and enjoy the story.
—P.E.

To Martha Seo and Setha Kang,
thanks for all your help!
—V.K.

Before you begin...

Math is real cool and reading is fun,
    So pay close attention—there's both to
    be done.

 As you read through this story, remember to look
For rhyming math problems contained in this
book.

These problems are fun but require your thought
About all that you learned and all you were taught.

So apply what you've learned from working in school.
These skills will make you—the coolest of cool!

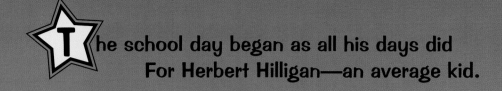 he school day began as all his days did
     For Herbert Hilligan—an average kid.

With his magical lunchbox—the coolest of cool—
     He ran down the street and on to his school.

Dressed like a cowboy, he just couldn't wait
     To learn about Texas—"The Lone Star State."

The subject that day was the Spindletop well—
     A high-shooting gusher with oil to sell.

It first gushed its oil in 1901,
     And even today its work is not done.

1.   For each single barrel which gushed from this well
      $5.00 a piece is the price each would sell.

      If Spindletop gushed a thousand barrels each day,
      After six days of gushing how much would you pay?

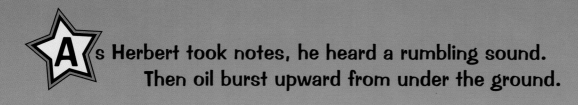
s Herbert took notes, he heard a rumbling sound.
Then oil burst upward from under the ground.

It shot Herbert up, away from his school,
Along with his lunchbox—the coolest of cool.

2.   For twelve seconds total Herbert flew through the air,
As the oil burst upward from under his chair.

If each single second he rose fifty feet,
How far in the air was he shot from his seat?

As the lunchbox popped open, a parachute came out
   To take Herbert and his dog on an uncertain route.

The Chihuahuan Desert is where they would land—
   A dry, rocky place with little or no sand.

This West Texas desert is large, vast, and great.
   It stretches from Mexico through the Lone Star State.

The temperatures can soar and the rainfall is low,
   But at times each year this place gets snow!

Herbert saw cactus and rocks all around,
   And then heard a rattle and a fast, shaking sound.

The sound Herbert heard—that fast, rattling shake—
   Was a clear sign to him that he'd just met a snake!

With diamonds on its back, this snake was no jewel,
   So Herbert used his lunchbox—the coolest of cool.

---

3. This dry, arid desert has temperatures that change—
    The low and the high have an eighty-degree range.

    If twenty-nine degrees is the temperature's low,
    How hot will it get, how high will it go?

4. The diamondback snake can attack with a bite.
    The sound of its shake will give you a fright!

    If every two minutes it rattles in power,
    How many times does this happen per hour?

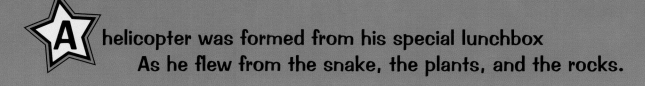

A helicopter was formed from his special lunchbox
As he flew from the snake, the plants, and the rocks.

Through the West Texas region, Herbert flew through the sky
Observing tall mountains he quickly passed by.

He flew east from El Paso, in a fast-moving streak,
Toward the highest point in Texas—Guadalupe Peak.

From there he went south; his direction would change.
He flew by the tops of the Davis Mountain range.

Continuing south to the park in Big Bend
Atop the Chisos Mountains, his flying would end.

5. Guadalupe Peak nears the sun's warming heat,
Standing eight thousand seven hundred fifty-one feet.

Comparing this to a mile in overall height,
How much of a difference would you sit down and write?

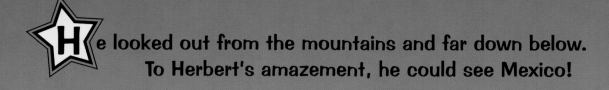He looked out from the mountains and far down below.
To Herbert's amazement, he could see Mexico!

The country borders Texas, but he remembered some more:
The states bordering Texas are a total of four.

Louisiana to the east and New Mexico west—
Herbert had just learned this for a geography test.

Oklahoma is big; it's vast and it's great.
It borders the north of the Lone Star State.

Arkansas is the last but certainly not least,
As it borders Texas from the nearby northeast.

Herbert heard thunder, which was threatening and loud.
He got drenched to the bone by the rain from the cloud.

---

6. The states bordering Texas are a total of four.
   Add Texas to this to count up one more.

   Of all fifty states, which are easy to count,
   These five southern states are what fractional amount?

7. The rainstorm was strong and showed its great power—
   3/4 of an inch came down in each hour.

   If it rained for three hours, think with your brain:
   What is the amount of overall rain?

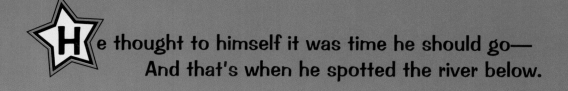

He thought to himself it was time he should go—
    And that's when he spotted the river below.

Because being safe is his number-one rule
    He threw out his lunchbox—the coolest of cool.

Instead of lifting off as a flying aircraft
    The lunchbox became a big rubber raft.

The thrill of this ride gave Herbert a shiver!
    He slid down the mountain to the Rio Grande River.

The Rio Grande runs at a fast, steady rate
    And borders the west of the Lone Star State.

Two other rivers you shouldn't forget
    Also form borders which are slippery and wet.

To the north is Red River; to the east the Sabine.
    If you look on a map these two can be seen.

8. He moved like a streak down this tall mountainside.
    This fast-moving thrill was a one-minute ride.

    If each single second he moved eighty feet,
    How tall was this mountain beneath Herbert's seat?

9. A kilometer's distance is a half-mile long—
    "Approximately" speaking this wouldn't be wrong.

    If 1,200 miles is the Rio Grande's size,
    How many kilometers would you see with your eyes?

s the rain made the current run fast, quick, and strong
It carried young Herbert swiftly along.

At the end of the river, known as its mouth,
Was the big Gulf of Mexico, which sits to the south.

It was cloudy and dark, but was raining no more,
As the saltwater waves pushed him to shore.

As he walked on the beach with lunchbox in hand
He saw something pointy in the grainy, wet sand.

Herbert knelt to the sand with his hand out to reach
And picked up a starfish that sat on the beach.

This single starfish that lay by itself
Herbert thought would look nice at home on his shelf.

10. The Rio Grande River was quick, fast, and strong.
     Three minutes per mile, Herbert rafted along.

     To raft sixty miles, moving this speed,
     How many hours do you think he would need?

11. Every two minutes a wave hit the sand
     Coming out from the ocean and reaching the land.

     If you count up the waves thinking this way,
     How many would come in one single day?

12. This starfish he found was real and alive.
     It had points all around, which totaled to five.

     The points on this starfish number the same
     As a five-sided shape called by what name?

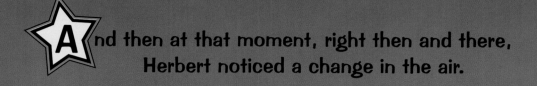**A**nd then at that moment, right then and there,
    Herbert noticed a change in the air.

He looked to the clouds with fear in his eyes
    As a fierce hurricane ripped through the skies!

It churned up the waves as it blew with a wrath.
    Herbert soon realized he was stuck in its path.

This powerful wind carried grass, dirt, and twigs—
    It made Herbert think of the three little pigs.

He thought of that story he had learned back in school
    And held out his lunchbox—the coolest of cool.

He wasted no time—his action was quick—
    As the lunchbox became a house made of brick.

It protected young Herbert from the hurricane's power
    But was plucked from the ground, like a bluebonnet flower.

The strong, violent winds made a loud, roaring sound
    As Herbert's brick house flew high off the ground.

13. The hurricane was fierce and moved really fast.
Each single second, one hundred feet passed.

   In two thousand feet it would hit Herbert's face—
So when would it reach him going this pace?

14. This house made of brick was shaped like a square.
It twirled all around as it moved through the air.

   If this sturdy brick house was ten feet per side,
How many square feet did the floor have inside?

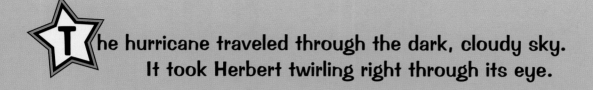

The hurricane traveled through the dark, cloudy sky.
It took Herbert twirling right through its eye.

It lost all its speed as it came to a stop
And set Herbert down on a building rooftop.

He stood on this roof, which was part of his school,
Holding his lunchbox—the coolest of cool.

The adventure he took was a wild, fun ride!
But school was in session, so he ran down inside.

The school bell that sounded was the regular call
For lunch to begin in the room down the hall.

---

15. This hurricane's winds spun Herbert around
    Five circles per second, high off the ground.

    If you count up the circles or revolutions per minute,
    How many would happen with Herbert trapped in it?

16. The hurricane's winds made a loud, scary sound
    As they carried young Herbert ninety feet from the ground.

    If the roof of the school was thirty feet high,
    How many feet did he drop from the sky?

17. He got back to school, and was glad to arrive,
    For lunch was to begin at 11:05.

    If he left school that morning at a quarter till 8:00,
    How long was his trip through the Lone Star State?

Herbert sat at the table and started to eat,
    And he found a surprise, a wonderful treat!

The pointy starfish, which was not big in size,
    Was staring young Herbert right in his eyes.

A golden light brown, like the color of toast,
    This single starfish was from the Gulf Coast.

This lone, single find made Herbert feel great—
    "The Lone Starfish of Texas," from his wonderful state.

18.   Herbert was thrilled by what he soon found—
      A five-pointed starfish weighing one-half a pound!

      If gathering starfish under the sun,
      How many are needed to equal one ton?

19.   If the starfish had babies, they would have to be small—
      Each one with five points and twenty in all.

      If you look at this family and find an amount,
      How many points would you most likely count?

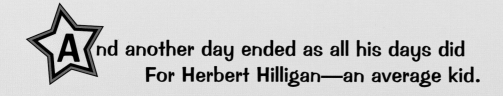

And another day ended as all his days did
For Herbert Hilligan—an average kid.

Just an average day for Herbert at school
And his magical lunchbox—the coolest of cool.

20. Through the air and on water his adventure was fun—
Nine hundred ten miles before he was done.

Seventy miles per hour and driving this far
Would take him how long if going by car?

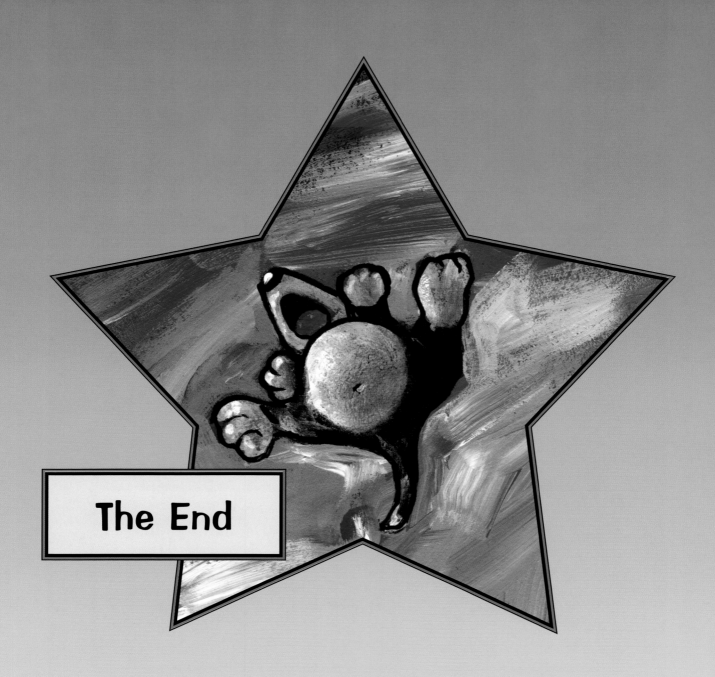

The End

Answers to Math Problems

1. $30,000

2. 600 feet

3. 109 degrees

4. 30 times per hour

5. 3,471 feet

6. 1/10

7. 2 1/4 inches

8. 4,800 feet

9. 2,400 kilometers
   ("approximately")
   *Note: a kilometer is
   "actually" .6 or 6/10
   of one mile, so the
   exact answer would
   be 2,000 kilometers

10. 3 hours

11. 720 waves

12. pentagon

13. 20 seconds

14. 100 square feet of
    space

15. 300 revolutions per
    minute

16. 60 feet

17. 3 hours 20 minutes

18. 4,000 starfish

19. 100 points
    (not counting Mom)
    105 points
    (counting Mom)

20. 13 hours

About the Author

Though he was born in New York, Paul Epner grew up in the Lone Star State and considers himself a native Texan.

At a young age, Paul caught Texas "rodeo fever" and decided to ride "buckin' broncos." Paul competed in many rodeos, and in several cases finished first, bringing home huge amounts of prize money and over-sized belt buckles.

One day, while riding "Whirlwind Willie," Paul was thrown from his horse and landed on his head. Luckily, he was not seriously injured; however, upon standing up, Paul started making up and solving math problems about everything he saw. When it came time to ride again, Paul felt his true calling was to be a middle-school math teacher. To this day, Paul credits the blow to his head as the sole reason why he decided to teach math in a middle school.

Today, Paul lives in San Antonio, Texas, with his wife, Susan, his beautiful, adorable, charming daughter, Allison, and his two "rodeo dogs," Shirley and Chester.

Vuthy Kuon ('wood-TEE kwon') has been featured on **NBC**, **ABC**, **CBS**, and **FOX**. He is the illustrator and author of the popular children's book *Humpty Dumpty: After the Fall*, and has illustrated other books including *Modern Day Fairy Tales* and *The Adventures of Roopster Roux*. This is his eighth book.

Born in Phnom Penh, Cambodia, Vuthy moved to the United States in 1975. Vuthy graduated with honors from the Rhode Island School of Design, where he studied under David Macaulay, Barry Moser, and Mary Jane Begin. He has worked at the Museum of Fine Arts, Houston, and the Children's Museum of Houston before becoming an art teacher. He currently lives in Houston, where he spends most of his time painting, playing golf, and speaking to schools across the country.

To see more of his artwork, go to his website:
www.woodtee.com
To schedule a school presentation, contact:
Vuthy Kuon • 1317 Ben Hur • Houston, Texas 77055
888.966.3833

Duke Nguyen ('wynn') is the son of a Vietnamese immigrant and an American mother. Born in Dallas and raised in Houston, Duke earned a degree at the University of Texas at Austin in advertising.

Before devoting himself to children's books, Duke worked for five years as an award-winning advertising copywriter in San Francisco and New York.

Before co-illustrating the Herbert Hilligan series, Duke began his career as a children's book writer. He is best known for his book *Elmer the Dog*, which was his first full-length book.

Duke's first published work was a story entitled *If a Carrot and Lettuce Raced*, featured in *The Rolling Stone and Other Read Aloud Stories*.

To schedule a school presentation, contact:
Duke Nguyen • 1232 Peden, #2 • Houston, TX 77006
713.861.5383

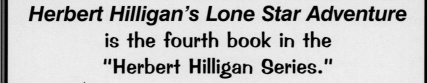